The First Sign of Winter

By Mary Blount Christian

Illustrated by Beverly Komoda

Parents' Magazine Press/New York

Text copyright © 1973 by Mary Blount Christian
Illustrations copyright © 1973 by Beverly Komoda
All rights reserved
Printed in the United States of America

Library of Congress Cataloging in Publication Data
Christian, Mary Blount.
   The first sign of winter.
   SUMMARY: Mama—looking for mittens, scrubbing the
storm windows, and taking Craig ice skating—is really
the first sign of winter.
   [1. Winter—Fiction]   I. Komoda, Beverly, Illus.
II. Title.
PZ7.C4528Fi   [E]   73-1066
ISBN 0-8193-0671-1
ISBN 0-8193-0672-X (lib. bdg.)

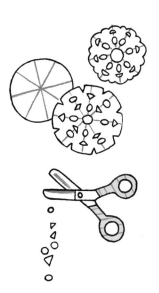

To my husband, Chris

The first sign of winter at Craig's house is Mama.
Before the first golden leaf falls from the tree,
he finds Mama in a dark corner of his closet.
"I must find matching mittens," Mama says.
But she never does.

Before the first gray and misty day,
Mama makes little piles of wooly clothes
all around Craig's room.
"These are too thin. These are too small.
These must be mended. These are just right," she says.

CLANK! CLANK! RATTLE! RATTLE!
Daddy is looking for snow chains for his car.
"You can't be too early," Daddy says.

He hangs them by the garage door.
"Find my sled, too, Daddy," Craig says.

Daddy leans the snow shovel by the door.

Now it's storm-window time. Mama washes the top panes, and Craig washes the bottom ones. When he sprays the glass, little drops of mist hang on his eyelashes.

After Daddy hangs the storm windows,
he smiles at Craig and Mama.
"There! Everything is ready."

One morning Craig wakes up and he knows winter has come
while he slept.
There's a whiff of chilly air just like when he first opens
the refrigerator door.
Mama is there with his warm wooly slippers.
"Old Jack Frost is nipping at our door," she says.

There's a frosty cover on Craig's bedroom window.
Mama helps him write WELCOME WINTER!
on the glass.

Winter has chased all the leaves from the trees.
Craig can see the bird nests that he could not see
all summer.
"Look!" Mama says, pointing to a small clump
on a branch. "That must be the robin's nest."

The first sign of frozen ponds is Mama at the hall closet.
CLINK! CLANK! She is getting the ice skates.
"You can't be too early," Mama says.

The next day the pond is frozen and sparkling
in the bright sun. Mama holds Craig's hand
until his feet stop wobbling and turning.

The first sign of snow is Mama, too.
One night she gathers Craig's clothes.
She gets two of everything: two shirts,
two pants, two pairs of socks.

The next morning Mama wakes him.
"Get up, Craig! See what winter has brought us."

"Snow! Snow!" he shouts.

In his four mittens, four socks, two pants,
two shirts, his wooly cap, his coat and rubber boots,
Craig walks stiffly like a windup toy.

Daddy must go to work on a beautiful snowy day.
He waves and drives away.
The car smokes like an angry dragon.

Craig and his friends have snowball fights.
The snowballs explode into soft little flakes.
When he is hit, Craig yells, "Ohhhhhhh,"
and falls into the soft snow.
He is not really hurt.

Now he falls back into the snow
and stretches his arms high above his head.
When Craig pulls them back to his sides,
he makes angel prints.
"I have wings. I can fly!" he shouts.

Craig plays alone when no one can play with him.
He builds a snowman.
He wraps Daddy's scarf around the snowman's neck.
"Hi, Daddy," Craig says
to his snowman. "How was work today?"

Inside the warm house, two of everything
hang over the radiator.
Two pairs of mittens, two pairs of socks,
two shirts, two pants, making puddles of water
on the floor.
The smell of warm wet wool tickles Craig's nose.

Then the sky turns a sad, dull gray.

The snow is gray and slushy.

It trickles into tiny little rivers

that rush to the street and down the gutters.

"Good-bye Mr. Snowman. Good-bye snow," Craig whispers.

CLATTER! CLATTER!
Mama has the cookie cutters.
Gingerbread cookies!
Craig cuts cookies while Mama bakes.
THUMP! THUMP! THUMP!
His cookie cutters hit as he cuts out
stars and flowers and fat little men.

The icy rain hits the windows
while Mama reads books to Craig.

When she is busy, he draws pictures of their house, with smoke curling from the chimney.

Sometimes they look at the flowers they picked
last summer and pressed between the pages
of a big book.

Then one day before the first green leaf comes out,
Craig sees Mama in the dark corner of his closet.
"I found one blue tennis shoe and one white tennis shoe,"
Mama says. "I must find matching tennis shoes."

She never does.

"The birds will be back soon," says Mama. "They're the first sign of spring. Then the trees will be green again." But Craig knows that Mama is really the first sign of spring.

Mary Blount Christian was born in Houston, Texas, where she still lives. Only a few years ago, she experienced her first major snowfall; now every Christmas she and her husband and children "go for snow." They drive until they find it and then enjoy sledding, making snowballs and snow ice-cream. One hot day, trying to conjure up the feeling of cold and snow, she wrote *The First Sign of Winter*. She is a graduate of the University of Houston and has worked as a reporter and columnist as well as a freelance writer. Currently, she reviews books for the *Houston Post*.

Beverly Kiku Komoda was born in Seattle, Washington, and grew up in State College, Pennsylvania. She met her husband Kiyo, who is also an illustrator, at the Chouinard Art Institute in Los Angeles, where they were both studying. She hoped to have a career in the cartoon field after graduation; eventually, however, she turned to book illustration which she found more to her liking. And for Parents' Magazine Press, she has illustrated *Jellybeans for Breakfast*, *Eighteen Cousins*, and *The Revolt of the Darumas*. The Komodas and their children live in New Jersey.